The Littlest Leprechaun

Written by
Brandi Dougherty

Illustrated by
Michelle Lisa Todd

Scholastic Inc.

For Oslo, my little leprechaun —B.D.

To my good friend Ian. Thank you for all your support. — M.L.T.

ISBN: 978-0-545-81089-0

16 15 21 22 23 24

Printed in the U.S.A. 40

First printing 2016

Liam was a leprechaun.
He lived with his family in the Enchanted Forest.
There were many leprechauns in Liam's village,
and they were all little.

But Liam was the littlest one.

It was a beautiful day, but Liam was bored.
He was tired of spending time playing hide-and-seek with his shadow.

He wanted to have a big, important job!

So Liam went to his dad's cobbler shop.
His dad made shoes for leprechauns near and far.
It was a very important job.

Liam's dad showed him how to measure the leather for each pair of shoes.
But the tape measure was very long.
Soon, Liam was all tangled up!
"Why don't you try helping your mom at the foundry?" his dad said.

Liam skipped across the village to the foundry.
Every leprechaun family had a pot of gold at the end of the rainbow.
And Liam's mom made all the pots!
It was a very important job.

Liam tried to keep the fire going while his mom melted iron for a new pot. But Liam's hands were too small to carry enough wood,

and his legs were too short to run between the furnace and the woodpile.

Soon, the fire went out. "I think your brother and sister could use a hand," Liam's mom said gently.

Liam's brother and sister worked in the post office.
They sent letters and packages all over the Enchanted Forest.
It was a very important job.
"I can do this!" Liam said.

But when Liam tried to mail a pair of shoes, he sent himself, too!
"Maybe not," Liam's brother said, opening the box.
"You should go help Uncle Albie," his sister offered.

So Liam went to find Uncle Albie.
He was getting ready to take a load of gold to the family's pot at the end of the rainbow.
"Carrying gold is a very important job," Uncle Albie said.
Liam was excited.

There was just one problem.
The gold weighed more than Liam did!
"Sorry, wee fella," Uncle Albie said.
"You're just too little."

Liam wandered through the Enchanted Forest.
He kicked the dirt. He was sad.

Liam knew there had to be one important job
he could do, even if he was little.

Then Liam heard a commotion near the old oak tree.
A group of leprechauns was gathered around Clover, the baby unicorn.
Clover was little, just like Liam.
But the poor unicorn's leg was stuck inside a hole!

"We need to dig a bigger hole," said one leprechaun.
"We can't!" replied another. "The tree roots are in the way."
"What if we all pull together?" another leprechaun,
with a very long beard, suggested.
"We'll hurt her!" cried a fourth leprechaun.
"Well, we can't just stand around all day," huffed a grumpy leprechaun.

Liam peered into the hole.
Just then, he had an idea!

"I can help!" Liam shouted extra loud.
"You?" said the grumpy leprechaun. "You're too little."

"You need someone little!" Liam cried.
Liam reached his tiny hand into the hole and gently pushed away the root that was trapping the unicorn's leg.

Clover was free! She licked Liam's cheek to thank him.
Everyone cheered as Liam and Clover danced and jumped around.

(Well, everyone except
the grumpy leprechaun.)

Liam had saved the day.
He was the hero of the entire Enchanted Forest.
Clover the unicorn stood proudly by his side.

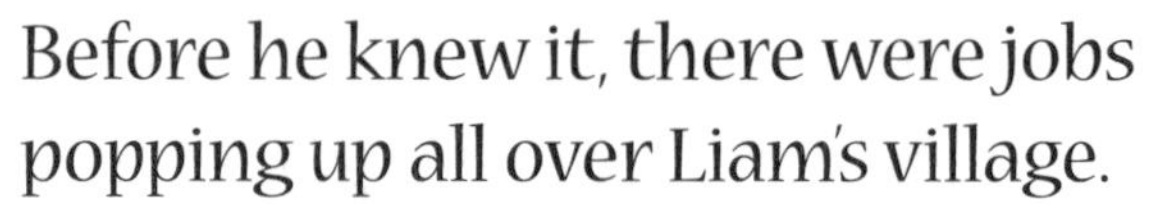

Before he knew it, there were jobs popping up all over Liam's village.

Everyone seemed to need a *little* extra help.

And Liam and Clover were the perfect size.

Liam had found his big, important jobs after all.
But even better, he had also made a special friend!